To leaders like my grandmother,
Mary Espinoza, whose hands are always ready to help. —JT

To Ed, for being next to me from beginning to end. —SP

About This Book

The illustrations for this book were made with gouache, acrylic, and digital media. This book was edited by Nikki Garcia and designed by Véronique Lefèvre Sweet. The production was supervised by Patricia Alvarado, and the production editor was Annie McDonnell. The text was set in Bell MT Std, and the display type is Addison West Flat.

Text copyright © 2022 by Jennifer Torres • Illustrations copyright © 2022 by Sara Palacios • Photograph of Dolores Huerta copyright © Cathy Murphy/Getty Images • Cover illustration copyright © 2022 by Sara Palacios • Cover design by Véronique Lefèvre Sweet and Christine Kettner. • Cover copyright © 2022 by Hachette Book Group, Inc. • Hachette Book Group supports the right to free expression and the value of copyright. The purpose of copyright is to encourage writers and artists to produce the creative works that enrich our culture. • The scanning, uploading, and distribution of this book without permission is a theft of the author's intellectual property. If you would like permission to use material from the book (other than for review purposes), please contact permissions@hbgusa.com. Thank you for your support of the author's rights. • Little, Brown and Company • Hachette Book Group • 1290 Avenue of the Americas, New York, NY 10104 • Visit us at LBYR.com • First Edition: August 2022 • Little, Brown and Company is a division of Hachette Book Group, Inc. • The Little, Brown name and logo are trademarks of Hachette Book Group, Inc. • The publisher is not responsible for websites (or their content) that are not owned by the publisher. • Library of Congress Cataloging-in-Publication Data • Names: Torres, Jennifer, author. | Palacios, Sara, illustrator. Title: Lola out loud / by Jennifer Torres ; illustrated by Sara Palacios. Description: First edition. | New York : Little, Brown and Company, 2022. | Audience: Ages 4–8. | Summary: As Lola helps her mother at the family's hotel, she learns about compassion, social injustice, and how one voice can lead to change. Includes author's note on Dolores Huerta, a labor organizer who co-founded the National Farm Workers Association. • Identifiers: LCCN 2021016145 | ISBN 9780316530125 (hardcover) | Subjects: LCSH: Huerta, Dolores, 1930—Juvenile fiction. | CYAC: Huerta, Dolores, 1930– Mexican Americans—Fiction. | Social justice—Fiction. | Compassion—Fiction • Classification: LCC PZ7.T645648 Lo 2022 | DDC [E]—dc23 • LC record available at https://lccn.loc.gov/2021016145 • ISBN 978-0-316-53012-5 • PRINTED IN CHINA • APS • 10 9 8 7 6 5 4 3 2 1

LOLA OUT LOUD

Inspired by the Childhood of Activist Dolores Huerta

By Jennifer Torres

Illustrated by Sara Palacios

LB

Little, Brown and Company

New York Boston

Lola cranked open her window at Hotel Delano and leaned into the summer air thick with hustle and grit.

Horns squawked on the street outside.

Bicycle bells jangled.

Another cable car rattled to a stop. They came every thirty minutes and always right on time.

"We have guests!" Lola shouted.

She scrambled down the hall, stumbled
past Grandpa, and raced to the lobby…

…where Mama would be waiting with welcome-home warmth and a gleaming brass key. If their guests didn't have money, Mama would let them pay with tomatoes.

And if they didn't even have tomatoes? Pues, she would take a handshake and a promise, because Lola and her mama kept more than clean towels at Hotel Delano.

They kept their hearts open. They kept their sleeves
rolled up. They kept their hands ready to help.

But one thing Lola never could keep was quiet.

"Where did you come from?" she asked. "How long will you stay?"

"Lola, hush," Mama said, "and set the table, por favor."

Only, the *plink plink* of fork against knife reminded Lola of the choir room piano, and before long, she was singing into a spoon.

"Hush," Mama said, handing her a broom. "Didn't you notice that pile of dust? When you see a problem, fix it. Don't pretend it isn't there."

But the *swish swish* of the bristles was like the rustle of flamenco skirts, and soon…

Lola was stamping
and spinning across
the floor.

Mama flashed a fed-up frown. She plunked a sudsy bucket at Lola's feet. "Windows, por favor," she said, pointing upstairs.

Lola threw back her shoulders and lifted her chin.

But before she could march upstairs, Grandpa cleared his throat. "Lolita Siete Lenguas," he teased. Little Lola, Seven Tongues, all fighting to be heard.

"For now, you must keep quiet. Only, don't forget—" He leaned in closer. "Sometimes one strong voice is just what we need."

Lola wished she could bite all seven of those wild tongues. They gave her nothing but trouble, and now they'd gotten her stuck upstairs. No one to talk to but the nightstand. Not a sound but the *tick-tock*ing of the clock—until, on the street below, another cable car squealed. Every thirty minutes, and always right on time.

"Off!" the conductor barked. "No fare, no ride!"

Two more workers. This time a woman and also a girl. Two satchels tumbled off the car, *tha-thump tha-thump* behind them. They trudged up the street as the cable car joggled away.

No fare? Lola thought with a how-dare-he huff. "No *fair*!"
Only, she didn't just think it. She said it out loud.

From downstairs came Mama's better-watch-it
warning, "*Lola…*"
So Lola kept quiet. But she couldn't look away.

Where had they come from? Where would they stay?
She leaned out the window. "Wait!" she shouted.
The girl looked up.
Lola ducked inside.

They needed help, and Lola had nothing. Just seven tongues, gone still and silent. She wrung out her rag.

Then she remembered Grandpa's words. "Sometimes," he had said, "one strong voice is just what we need."

A take-a-chance twinkle lit up her eyes.

She had seven tongues all fighting to be heard.

She ran downstairs. Her steps were as sure as any she had ever danced.

She pounded on the guest room doors. "*¡Vamos!* While we can still catch up!" Her voice was as clear as any note she ever sang in the choir room or kitchen.

She darted down the hall—straight into Mama.

A here-we-go-again "Hush!" hovered on Mama's tongue.

But Lola's was quicker.

She explained what she had seen: the conductor and the cable car. Another mama, another girl.

"If you see a problem, fix it!" Lola burst out.
"Don't pretend it isn't there."

Mama opened her mouth, not "Hush!" this time, but *"Hurry!"* She flew to the kitchen, set two more places at the table.

The guests marched after Lola.

Grandpa called out from the door,
"Can one brave voice lead the way?"

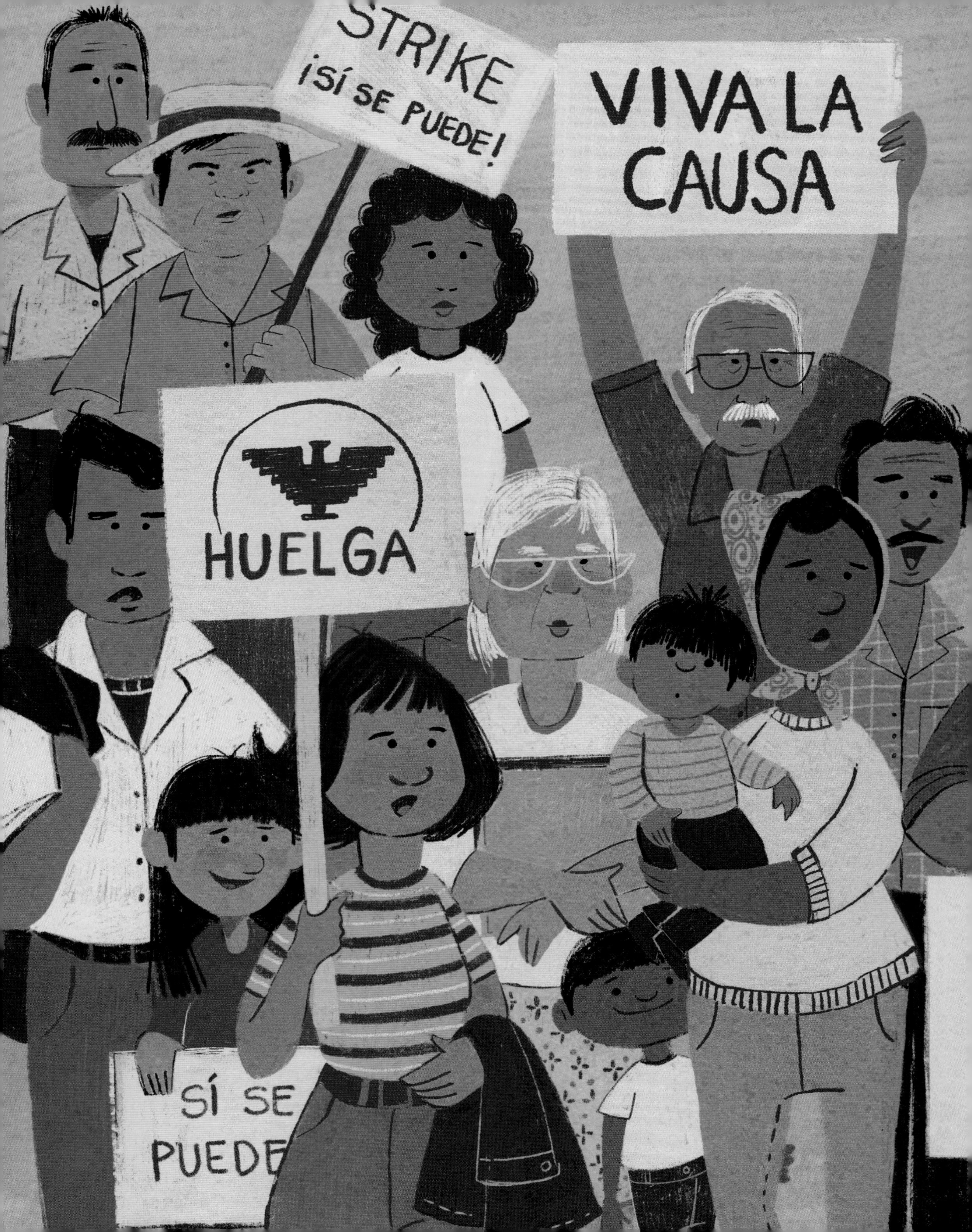
STRIKE
¡SÍ SE PUEDE!
VIVA LA CAUSA
HUELGA
SÍ SE PUEDE

"¡Sí se puede!" Lola shouted years later, loud as seven tongues all cheering. "Yes it can!" Her heart was open. Her sleeves were rolled up. Her hands were ready to help.

UNITED FARM WORKERS

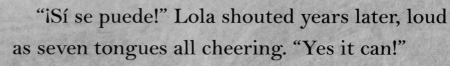

Author's Note

• • • • • • • • • • •

This imagined story was inspired by the real childhood of Dolores Huerta—Lola is a nickname for Dolores. Alongside Cesar Chavez, she went on to champion the rights of farmworkers and their families, eventually founding the United Farm Workers union, which was based in a small town called Delano in California's Central Valley.

Born in New Mexico, Dolores grew up in Stockton, California, where her mother, Alicia Chávez, owned a hotel that served mostly poor farmworkers. Dolores has said her first lessons in social justice came from watching the compassion with which her mother treated hotel guests, letting them pay in produce when they didn't have cash—sometimes letting them stay without paying anything at all.

Dolores was a Girl Scout. She sang in the church choir. She took violin lessons. She dreamed of becoming a famous flamenco dancer. Her grandfather, Herculano Chávez, helped raise her and her siblings, and really did nickname her Siete Lenguas, or "Seven Tongues," because she talked so much.

Later, Dolores went to college and became a teacher. She saw many of her students, the children of farmworkers, come to school hungry, often without shoes. She decided the best way for her to help the children was to help their parents fight for better pay and working conditions.

Dolores Huerta is perhaps best known for the phrase "Sí se puede," which translates as "Yes, it can be done," or "Yes, we can!" But my favorite Dolores Huerta quote comes from an interview she gave in 1974. Asked if she had ever felt unsure of herself, Dolores replied, "Of course. I've been afraid about everything until I did it. I started out every time not knowing what I was to do and scared to death." Lola reminds me that sometimes the biggest and bravest voices start out scared and uncertain. That one strong voice can lead the way. You can read more about Dolores Huerta and her work at DoloresHuerta.org.

Dolores Huerta speaks onstage during a United Farm Workers rally in California, in 1975 or 1976.